UNEXPECTED GUESTS

The inner beauty of love

By

Kiran Kumar.M.S

pencil

ISBN 978-93-5438-885-9
© KIRAN KUMAR.M.S 2020
Published in India 2020 by Pencil

A brand of
One Point Six Technologies Pvt. Ltd.
123, Building J2, Shram Seva Premises,
Wadala Truck Terminal, Wadala (E)
Mumbai 400037, Maharashtra, INDIA
E connect@thepencilapp.com
W www.thepencilapp.com

Author biography

My self KIRAN KUMAR. M. S. Doing my Under graduation and i write love stories more because i feel that love is most beautiful part of our life. Writing is just a hobby of mine.

Table of Contents

Unexpected guests... A beautiful love story

The new generation that is the upcoming generation will be not knowing the feelings. When we talk about the word feeling the first thing which strikes our mind is the word LOVE. Great, actually this word has a more weightage, its beyond our imagination, it's the purest form of feeling etc.

now a days it has no value everyone will scare when they listen the word LOVE, especially parents will scare to the peak when they come to know that their kids are in love. Why, why this happened? It's all because of our generation.

Now a day's love is all about lust. They don't know the difference between LOVE & LUST.

In future generation it will be ruined more and more. Now I am going to tell a story which is narrated to a 23 years old boy by his father. Lets get into the story.

This is the story from year 2040.

There is boy named AKARSH. His age is 23. Studying engineering, who is crazy about girls, who is expert in flirting. He doesn't know the emotions, feelings. In one word he is a playboy. His father named VEDANT who is one amongst top 10 richest person in state, married to DIYA. She is a typical Indian woman and a homemaker. Akarsh is the boy who dated many girls and he neither girls were never serious about any relationship so far. Once he met a girl named Aarohi she is very pretty and she is so friendly with everyone. Aarohi is a junior to Akarsh. And she didn't know the past life of Akarsh. During a college fest Akarsh saw Aarohi performing for a dance. He took a chance and made an appreciation for her performance. Akarsh got a chance to make friendship with her. As day passes, they exchanged numbers and started daily conversation. Text turned into calls and calls turned into video calls and as day passes meetings and outings has started. And slowly friendship converted into love. One fine day he made confession about his feelings and she took a time and accepted it as she didn't know about his past because he never shared with her. Everything was going fine and Akarsh completed his graduation he was not serious about his carrier because his father has much money. After his graduation he started to avoid Aarohi. She got confused about his behavior and finally without no reason he said a breakup for Aarohi.

It broke her heart and she went to depression and as a result she got failed in subjects. She couldn't able to digest her depression and failure and decided to end her life by committing suicide. She made an attempt to hang herself.

But is she lucky enough that her mother saw her hanging to fan and rescued her but it was bit late. She admitted to hospital, she was heavily injured around her neck and she had a laryngeal fracture, spine fracture, doctors informed that chances of being alive is less than 50%. She was kept in a ventilator and she is was in a death bed. Her father started to enquiry her friends to know the reason behind her suicide attempt. There he got to know about the breakup with Akarsh. He lodged an official complaint against Akarsh. Police began their enquiry and in no time, they arrested Akarsh. Vedant and diya had no idea about Akarsh arrest. Vedant used all his influence and got a bail for Akarsh.

After this Akarsh didn't understood one thing that how a girl can end her life for silly reason. Vedant came to know the stupid thing what Akarsh was doing till that day and he trashed him. He went to hospital to look the condition of Aarohi, it was very bad and he apologize to her parents. He convinced them and he shifted Aarohi to abroad for treatment, he took all the medical expenses and paid for it. Akarsh had one question left in his mind. And decided to ask her mother.

Akarsh: mom, I need to ask you one question which is bothering me after this incident.

Diya: ok ask me, I will answer.

Akarsh: mom, what is love? Is that so serious?

Diya: what you have done till today, that is not a love its only lust. You want to know the meaning of love? You want to know the depth of love? You want to know the purity of love? Go, ask your dad. You know one thing he is a not only a richest person but also, he is a greatest lover as I saw. Ask him he will explain you. He is so ashamed of you today. Being his son, you did like this.

Akarsh: sorry mom.

Akarsh waits for his father to return to home. He arrives, as soon as he arrived, he questioned his father.

Akarsh: Hai dad, I know you are ashamed of me, I am so sorry for what I did, I was not knowing that just breakup will be so serious.

Vedant : oh "just a breakup". You fool its not just. You don't know the meaning of love so it is "just" for you. No, my son it's not as easy as you think. Till today you didn't experience the true love so you don't know the effect of it. Don't repeat it in future.

Akarsh : no dad, I wont do it. But I wanted to know the real meaning of love, mom said to ask you. Can you please share that with me?

Vedant : Ok come here take a seat. Diya you too take your seat. Akarsh you wanted to know the real meaning of love right ok let me tell you. Did you ever tried to think why I am so rich? No of course you didn't I know. Its because of love. Yes, you heard right. Love is not just meeting a girl, hanging out, chatting etc etc… love is an inspiration, motivation, understanding, sacrificing, pain, happiness etc etc etc. Ok let me tell you a story.

Akarsh : a story, wow cool I am ready and excited to listen the story.

Vedant : no, not just a story. It's the secret of my life which I never wanted to share with anybody. Very few know my story and in that few it includes your mom. Today I share this with you. But you should not just listen, you have to imagine and feel the characters then only it is possible to understand the beautiful concept love. Akarsh : Ok dad, I am ready.

(30 years ago-2010)

When I was at your age, studying engineering I was so joy full person I had no reason to get sad. I was enjoying my life to fullest I had no tension and I am not a brilliant student just an average student who is managing to pass all the subjects. Life was going easy somehow, I completed my 1st year of engineering. As we enter the second year, we became a senior so we were going for 1st year block and making fun of students and ragging them in fun manner. There I got a twist in my life. I saw a girl standing in a corner with innocent face, and very scared of seniors. As soon as I saw I was unable to take my eyes from her. some kind of feeling started which I never experienced before. It called love at first sight.

Till I saw her I never believed the concept love at first sight. I was waiting to see her every day, I was waiting for my chance to talk with her. After a lot of research and struggle I got to know the name and branch. Her name was SARAH which means queen. Yes, she was like a queen.

Finally, I got a chance to talk with her after 4 months. I got a suggestion on facebook and I sent a friend request and she accepted. I wanted to text but my hands were freezing, I was unable to type but some how with all guts I texted her and got a reply. I was in cloud 9, I was so happy, no words are sufficient to describe my happiness on that time. I never wanted to stop conversation with her so I was texting her continuously and happy thing was I use to get a reply for my text.

This continued for about another 4 to 5 months. And decided to meet in college. Oh my god it was one of the best moments in my life. That night I didn't slept, I was waiting and waiting and waiting for sun watching clock continuously I was so excited. Finally, clock strikes 6 in the morning and sun was raising. I woke and started preparation to meet my queen sarah. Went to the college waiting for her near the cafeteria. I was there 1 hour before the decided time. I was well prepared to talk with her and had a fear that how to face her. I saw her arriving to cafeteria and in fear I hid behind the wall. She waited for 10 min and texted.

Sarha: hy Vedant where are you? I am waiting near cafeteria? are you busy right now?

Vedant: hello, I came to cafeteria 1 hour before but I scared to meet you and talk with.

Sarha: why are you so scared? Please don't make me embarrassed, come and take your seat.

With full of fear I went to her and took a seat. I greeted her with smile.

Sarha: are you okay now? Why are so scared, am I so ugly?

Vedant: hy no no no, you are gorgeous. The reason I am scared is I never talked with the girl before so.

Sarha: ohh ok its fine. I too never talked with the random guy this my first meet with a guy apart from class.

Vedant: so how the college life going on?

Sarha: yeah, it's good, how about you?

Vedant: yeah, its fine. How were your internals?

Sarha: can we please talk something out of academics?

Vedant: yeah sure, sure. I am sorry. I am tensed I don't know what to talk.

Somehow, I managed to talk with her we exchanged our thoughts and lifestyles and we exchanged a numbers. But never called her because I was a shy person. But I wanted share my feelings on her. I was waiting for a right time and texting continued for 2 years, even after 2 years I didn't get enough guts to say my feelings. I was scared of loosing her friendship too. I got my graduation completed.

I was knowing that if I leave college, I don't get a chance to see her in future and before leaving I wanted to see her one last time. I could have called her and ask to meet but I didn't because I was sure that I ending up in tears after saying an official goodbye to her. So, waited in the campus to see her after a long 1 hour waiting, she finally came to canteen, I was standing in one corner and watching her smile for one last time.

And as I said I ended up in tears and left her a message that I am busy so I couldn't meet her before going and said goodbye in text. Even after 3 years' time I couldn't express my feelings. I joined for higher studies but texting to her didn't stopped. After a year she completed her graduation too and got a job. Everything was going well and I left with one more year to complete my studies. Suddenly one morning I received a text.

Sarha: hai, I got engaged. Sorry I didn't invited you for an engagement because the exams are going on for you.

Vedant: hahaha…. stop kidding I know you are joking; you can't fool me.

Sarha: hy no, I am not kidding, I am serious.

Vedant: oh really, ok send me pics so that I can believe you.

Sarha: ok wait, see this is my fiancé.

[I received a bunch of pics] [I couldn't control my tears, I remained silent and staring her pics, cursing god]

Sarha: hy vedant you there?

[I dint replied her text because I was in shock and fear of losing her forever] After a lot of thinking finally decided to express my feelings to her I know it was already late but if I didn't try now, I know I will loose her forever. So, in the I called her.

Vedant: sarha, are you free now? I need to talk one important thing I need your time.

Sarha: yeah, I am free but is everything ok with you? Are you fine?

Vedant: yeah yeah, I am totally fine. I just wanted to say you the truth. Please meet me at river bed near our college, I am coming in 10 min its so urgent.

Sarha: yeah sure I will be there in 10 min. [I was waiting for her near river bed, she came and asked what happened] Vedant: Till today I just acted to be friend with you. I was never ready to be only friend with you. I can't loose you. I am nothing without you. [I went on my knees and confessed my love] look I waited for so many years for this right time. I don't know whether you will accept my love or not but I couldn't stop loving you. The first day when I saw you, right there I decided that you are my lifeline but I dint get a enough dare to confess, and if didn't tell you now I would end up by not expressing my feelings so I am confessing now please, will you accept my proposal?

Sarha: Vedant Look you are a very good friend of mine and you are an amazing person but you already know I got engaged. You have a bright future don't waste it. concentrate on your carrier. I wish to see you in very good position. Fullfill my wish please.

Vedant: what if I proposed before you getting engaged?

She left place by not answering my question. I cried and cried and cried on that day and I stopped texting her. It was very tough to avoid her but I have to do it. As she said I concentrated on my carrier to fullfull her wish and as a result I got placed in one of the top company with impressive salary package. I called to my parents and said about my placement they were so happy for me. After a long gap on that day I couldn't control so I texted.

Vedant: hai sarha, how are you?

Sarha: OMG, Vedant its been so long, I am good. How about you?

Vedant: yeah, I am good too. By the way I wanted to tell you that your wish is completed.

Sarha: My wish? What was that?

Vedant: your wish that you wanted to see me in good position, its fulfilled today. Thank you sarha for inspiring me. I am in this position because of my parents and you, thank you

Sarha: wow it's a great news we need to celebrate it and please stop being so dramatic ah. Saying thank you and all its more dramatic. I am so happy for you. I am bit busy I will call you tomorrow. Bye Like this again I started a conversation again and whenever I text her, I couldn't control my tears. Again, our daily conversation has started and again I was waiting for her call but I didn't receive any calls as usual she got busy with her work. But she was replying my text whenever she gets free time.

Finally, one day I got a call I was so happy and took a call. She said that she wants to meet so I dressed up and went to location where she already waiting for me.

Sarha: hai, was you busy, sorry I forgot to ask this before.

Vedant: no, I am never busy for my queen. Tell me what's the matter?

Sarha: vedant, you still waiting for me? Still loving me?

Vedant: [with vibrating voice] what type of question is this my queen? If you are in my mind I would have forgotten you by this time, but you are in my heart how can I forget my love towards you and fact is its increasing day by day and I will wait for you till my last breath, I know you don't have a feeling on me and I know I cant marry you but also I will wait for you.

Sarha: can you make one promise for me? Its last please

Vedant: anything for you my queen. If you will be happy from that promise then I wont event think twice to make a promise.

Sarha: few days ago, I met your mom and she explained about your decision and about your condition. You made a decision that you won't get marry? Please take back that decision and you have to get marry you made a promise and you can't break it.

Vedant: ok done I said anything for you, and I am ready to get marry. Its very difficult for me but all will be happy right if I changed my decision. Ok fine I am ready.

Sarha: thank you so much your mom already searched a girl for you and I already talked with her. We all liked her so tomorrow you are going to meet her.

Vedant: cool, ok fine.

Sarha: and one more thing very important after meeting her just meet me you have a surprise.

Vedant: ok fine done……

The next morning I went to meet a girl and I received a text from Sarha saying all the best..

Vedant: hai, I am Vedant how are you?

Diya: hai, I am Diya I am fine and nice to meet you…

Vedant: mom said that you liked me so straightly I will come to the point. I was loving one girl of course I am loving her now and I will do it in future you should not put any restriction.

Diya: she is Sarha right. Yeah she said everything about you and your feelings towards her and infact I liked you for that reason. You loved her beyond your ego, self respect, now a days this kind of love is quite rare and I am happy that I met that kind of person. I respect your feelings and I wont disturb them even in future. And about me I had no bad past nothing just simple living girl.

Vedant: are you sure? If yes then its good. Our parents will talk the further things. I take a leave now bye..

Diya: yeah I am sure. And I will be waiting to see us on our wedding album. Bye take care

After that all I was waiting for my surprise and Sarha came but she looked quite disturb.

Vedant: hai sarha,

Sarha: hai Vedant.

Vedant: why so late?

Sarha: sorry I was stuck in traffic, by the way how was the meeting?

Vedant: yeah it went good and I am doing this all only for you.

Sarha: thank you…. i am sure you will be happy in future.

Vedant: today you are looking so disturbed. What happened? Is everything fine?

Sarha: yeah yeah everything fine…

Vedant: so what's the surprise? I am waiting..

Sarha: [she handed over her wedding card to me] this is the surprise my wedding on coming month…..

Vedant: [tears started to roll down, I hid my tears controlled very hard] ohh wow cool it's a good news…I am happy for you….i am so excited…

Sarha: Vedant please stop acting I know you are not happy I can see your tears in your eyes so please control yourself. I am sorry vedant please don't spoil your life by remembering me. You have a beautiful life enjoy it. I don't want to see your life getting spoiled. Forget everything and move on.

Vedant: move on? Its so easy to say this word Sarha but its not gonna happen because I loved you with my whole heartedly and I am so serious about you. And you tell me to forget everything…. how? I don't understand how can I unfeel love once I have felt it? How can I forget that which gave me so much to remember? There is quote that "one bad chapter doesn't mean that the story is over" they say but why cant they understand that its difficult to turn the page when you know that someone wont be in the next chapter?

Sarha: but what about your future, what about you? I am scared about your future.

Vedant: why you are so scared? If you are happy then I will be happy. You smile when you are happy and I smile when I see you happy.

Sarha: I am scared because I LOVED YOU TOO

Vedant: what, what did you just say?

Sarha: yes you heard me right. I fell in love with you. How I can not love you when you are showing me so much love care respect. But I can't have you in my life. My mom wanted me to get marry with this boy and I don't like him, they didn't even asked me before engagement, didn't asked me before printing the wedding cards, and I am sure they wont ask me even now. Nobody wants my opinion. And I wont make my parents feel sad by stopping this marriage because they are everything for me. Till today they have done and sacrificed much for me and I owe them so I decided to get marry. But believe me I loved you the way you loved me.

Vedant: shall talk with them. Come lets go. I will explain them everything.

Sarha: no, its already too late and I don't want to hurt them now. Please can you sacrifice your love for sake of my parents.

Vedant: do you know how much I loved you? I can do anything for you and I can sacrifice my love for you. I want only one thing from you. Your happiness that's enough. I will do anything for your happiness you know that.

Sarha: I am sorry Vedant. Please take care.bye

And after this there was no conversation between us for month and one she texted me to come to marriage a week before. As she said I went a week before and she was happy.

[The night before marriage day we were talking in wedding hall]

Vedant: how's the preparation going on? Your parents will be very happy today.

Sarha: yes, they are happy.

Vedant: this is place where I wanted to sit and tie a knot around your neck. But tomorrow someone will sit on that place. From tomorrow you are wife to him. And there will no good morning, good night messages, I can't talk to you, I cant hear your voice, I cant make you smile I am going to miss you, miss your smile, miss your voice.

Sarha: I miss you too.

The time has come and she came and sat with him. She was looking gorgeous and I was staring her I couldn't take my eyes out of her. And again I fell in love with her. Every single moment we spent, we discussed was striking my head and I can see the first day when I met her infront of eyes. Then I realized that day dreaming is true, I experienced that. I was looking at her and all of the sudden she collapsed and everyone gathered around her but she was unconscious. I was blank I don't know what was happening. Her father came to me and said to drive her to hospital and I took my car and she was lying unconscious in back seat I took her to hospital with her parents and took her to emergency ward after some time doctors came out and said SHE IS NO MORE. Doctor explained that She died because of heart attack. It happens when people get depressed and when they can't handle the pain the heart stops the working.

By hearing this news, I collapsed on ground. After cremation I went to their house collected all her memories and asked her parents.

Vendant: are you happy now? You killed your daughter. Do you know that? You are the murders. you killed my love my Sarha. Why didn't you asked her before fixing her marriage? If you did then she would be alive now. Can you bring her back?

I cried daily for her. My room was filled with her pics and memories and when heart get too heavy with pain people just turn silent, completely silent. And after this all I married to diya as it was wish of sarha and we are happy together now but even now I didn't stop loving her. (Present day-2040) I still have that car in my garage and i can still see her on back seat. So my son this was the story of my love life which I loved her to the death and I couldn't get her. So respect the love, breakup is not a small matter.

Akarsh: now I realized that the true meaning of love. Dad can I see Sarha pics?

Vedant: come with me. See this is the secret of mine where nobody is allowed here. Today I am showing you. Look at this I created all her memories here and when I ever get sad, I spend some time with her.

Akarsh: dad I want to meet Aarohi. I will go to hospital.

[In hospital]

Akarsh: sorry uncle I made a big mistake how is she now? Aarohi's dad: [slapped Akarsh] she is still alive. Now please go out from here

Akarsh: i deserve this uncle but believe me I understood my mistake and came here to confess my mistake. Please allow me

[Aarohi from inside says "dad allow him"]

Akarsh: I am sorry Aarohi this was all because of me I won't repeat it please give me another chance to correct my mistakes. She allowed him to correct his mistake and now there are happily married and they blessed with the baby girl and named her as SARHA.

So a true love story is based on compromise, trust, respect. The pure love is when your smile because of someone, its special feeling. But when you cry for someone it's a love.

You are so lucky if u receive first and last message of the day from same person. Every smile never shows a love but every drop from your eyes shows a trusted love.

So the meaning of title "the unexpected guest" here there are 3 unexpected guest.

1) Aarohi suicide: Akarsh didn't expected it. 2) Sarha: sarha entering the life of vedant. 3) Sarha death

These are "unexpected guest" in this story. So find your love. I am sure it will be so beautiful and it makes your life beautiful. Many peoples says bad things about love they talk when they don't deserve that or when they don't know the value of that.

As i said love is the inspiration it happened in vedant life. She inspired him to get into good position and she is the reason he is living his life and when comes to the sacrifice they both sarha and vedant sacrificed their love for her parents sake. And when comes to understanding divya did it well. When she knows everything about their love life but also she understood him and believed him and got married to him..

So the only message i like to convey through this story is love with your whole heart. Not with your hole heart. And parents, ask your daughter or son before fixing the marriage because they have lead their rest of the life with the life partners. Thank you all… A small story by KIRAN KUMAR.M.S

Here are some other stories of mine hope you like it.

1] TITLE : "SHE" "SHE"

The word "SHE" has more respect and everyone knowns the popular saying that there is no HE without SHE. Yes its very much true. She has a more importance in every HE.

Here is something I tried to put up in words that what changes will be in HE when SHE enters in his life. Let me tell it in a simple story. I prefer a lovestory because it is more easy to connect. Lets begin with the story.

Once upon a time there is one boy whose nature is so careless and lack of feelings but he was a joyful person. He don't know the pain of loosing something which is more importing thing or most loved thing because his parents made him so comfortable with the things he loved. Ofcourse every parents will do the same or try to do there best.

And a girl whose nature is so friendly and very matured minded she knows what to pick or what to choose. She came over all the situation and became so strong. Yes ofcourse she so adorable.

The characters journey begins in college. After there 10th they join to PUC where everyone are strangers on the first day, as the time passes and day passes they become friends likewise the my story characters become friends day by day they become more close and begins to share everything. Due to her simplicity and nature the boy fell in love with her.

When the boy fell in love with her he doesn't know that he gonna experience the new kind of feelings. Once he starts liking her he feel jealous when ever someone talk with her closely. Before that he is never jealous about anyone or anything. And when he approached her about his feelings she denied because she is mature she knows what to select. She doesn't want to convert her friendship into love. The boy gets sad and starts to shed his tears which doesn't came from almost 5-8 years. But he didn't loose hope and kept on trying. And kept on building his expectation. He don't know that his own expectation make him hurt in future. He begins to miss her every single second. He don't want to force her for relationship and on same he don't want to loose her. He slowly starts to learn the face of sadness which he never saw before. He starts to respect the women more even before. At some point of time he begins to loose his confident on her and tries to give up and become normal like before. But it was too late. How do one say goodbye when your heart still wants to hold on?

His excitement was seeing her, his happiness was talking with her, his fear was losing her. As the day passes his eyes getting more and more tears. "THE RAIN FALLS BECAUSE THE CLOUDS CAN NO LONGER HANDEL THE WEIGHT, AND TEARS FALLS BECAUSE THE HEART CAN NO LONGER HANDEL THE PAIN." Its feels funny for many peoples when they see boys shed there tears. But he is the only one who knows what he is going through. He doesn't want other people to notice his wet eyes especially his parents. So He put on a fake smile on his face. She never ignored him he felt ignored because the time she is giving for him was not meeting his expectation timing. Our heart needs more time to accept the truth which our mind knows already. He understands that and also he understood that "IF YOU TRULY LOVE SOMEONE, THEN THE ONLY THING YOU WANT FOR THEM IS TO BE HAPPY, EVEN IF ITS NOT WITH YOU."

From this short story we can see that the important role of "SHE" in "HE" life. She unknowingly thought many things which is more important for every human beings. If you didn't notice what she thought in his life I listed them below. She thought him what is true love. She thought him the pain of missing something which is loved most. She thought him a life lesson that forever happiness is not possible. She thought him to stop expectation. She thought him never make somone so special because small changes can hurt more. She thought him to respect women. She thought him to be mature. She thought him sacrificing. She thought him the joy of missing the person we love. She thought him to accepting the truths and so on…………….. Do you remember your childhood, we cry loudly to get what we love but when we grow up we cry silently to forget what we love and "SHE" is so strong in this. They can sacrifice anything.

Mens are not toys they too having a feelings but not as much as women's. everyone gets sad but thing is who covers it better from world and answer is womens yes they are more stronger than men……….

▪▪▪

TITLE 2

"2020" THE MOST UNDER RATED YEAR

Hello everyone, this article is based on the year 2020.I wish to ask one common question to everyone. "how was your year 2020?"

yes, I can hear your answers. Everyone is saying like:

"it's the worst year we have ever seen"

"it's the most difficult year"

"it's the horrible year". Etc etc etc………..

Ok fine, the next question rise is why it's the worst year?

I know you give the reasons like "due to lockdown, due to corona, due to natural calamities something and something else…ok I agree with your reasons. But I try to change your opinion on "2020."

According to me the year 2020 is the best thing I ever saw. You guys confused?... ok I explain it.

Before talking about the year 2020 let us rewind our time that is before 2020. How it used to be the years before 2020. Take a look, where were you? what were you doing? whom you were missing?

The answers for this are IT company employees are spending most of their time in office, school and college students were spending their most of time in classes, hostel students are staying in hostel. When I mention this, you guys will say that we were also enjoying the parties, outing, trips and movies. Yes, I agree we were enjoying but did you guys ever thought of your parent's wife children siblings. Were you guys available for them? No all were busy in their private life enjoying the stuff outside the home. We were a machines before the 2020. We all programmed to do our work. Apart from work nothing else. We rarely sat with parents and talked about our things we rarely took care of our loved ones its all because of our busy life schedule.

We were talking on the phone calls while having breakfast lunch dinner. Thinking about projects, meetings, works etc…. planning weekends with the friends of course rarely with families. But parents were thinking all the time about their children, wife thinking about her husband. Don't they deserve our time. We were just leading a robotic life.

Then comes the year 2020. The new virus begins to spread all over the world. All countries begin to shut down the cities. The mechanical world, the robotic world has shut down completely. No more competition, no more running for work, no more running for classes. How we spent our lockdown? By staying in home, by spending time with our parents, with children, with loved ones. We spent time by watching movies with family, we spent time by talking to our parents, we spent time by cooking with mother, we shared our thoughts and love completely in this lockdown period. We all spent some quality time with family.

Just think you were waking up in the morning without any tension about work, projects, meeting. As soon as you woke, you walk to kitchen, there mother cooking breakfast and make a greeting to you with a warm hug and smile with pure love. After preparing breakfast having it with whole family on one table. Has this ever happened before? We all running for work we didn't have a time to ask parents about their breakfast lunch dinner and their health. Many of you missed the food being feed by mother. Due to this lockdown it gave us a opportunity to know that feeling. At the snacks time discussing what to prepare for snacks and taking a part in preparing snacks and helping parents in household work. And the lovers chatting most of the time in a day like never before and playing games with family after our snacks. Isn't this life beautiful than before. If you didn't notice the change in parents or lover or the person who tries to talk with you from before and now you make a time for them. Ask those peoples, they never going to say it's a worst year.

Yes, it may be difficult to stay in home without going outside or without parties which we all are addicted. But the truth is its more worth

The losses have occurred for lower class people, many lives lost but we can't blame the year 2020. It may be loss in money or in profit but we gain much like happiness of family, the feelings of our loved ones, the quality time with family. Does the parties, trips, movies are more important than family. No, not at all. We were not aware of this thing. The year 2020 thought this big lesson to all of us.

At your younger age let's say when you were 6 years old. You woke up 6;30 AM and it's raining outside. Mom told you to not attend school today, you are under blanket, you are watching rain through your window. You sit on your bed and turn on tv, your mom made you breakfast, you are watching cartoons. Life was so good right at that age. Now in the year 2020 is no difference. It gave your childhood happiness back. And all are cursing the year 2020.

When it comes to natural calamities, yes those were the disasters. But the natural calamities happened only in the year 2020. Didn't it happen before? Why natural calamities occurred or occurring? It's because for the action of humans on nature. We never cared about our nature except on June 5th. We used our nature like anything. Because of our action on nature it giving a reaction. Its nothing but a KARMA that's it simple. And the main thing about 2020 is our nature has healed it self much without pollution of vehicles.

Finally, according to me the year 2020 is best year which we never saw before. It has thought us a very important lesson. It gave us a break from our busy schedule. How many are missing those days I don't know. But I am going to miss those days very badly. I think it never comes in future.

I tried to change the peoples thought on year 2020 through this small article. I don't know how you feel after reading this article. And I don't know what personal reason you guys have to hate this year. But I don't have a single reason to hate 2020.

.............END..............

If you are missing someone at this time just feel these quotes. THESE ARE SOME COLLECTIONS:

1] MISSING SOMEONE WHO IS MISSING YOU TOO IS SWEET PAIN, BUT MISSING SOMEONE WHO IS NOT MISSING YOU AT ALL IS SLOW DEATH. 2]

THE HARDEST THING TO DO IS WATCH THE ONE YOU LOVE, LOVE SOMEONE ELSE.

3] ITS FUNNY HOW THE ONE YOU NEED DOESNT NEED YOU, HOW THAT ONE PERSON BROUGHT OUT THE BEST AND WORST IN YOU, HOW THE ONLY PERSON WHO CAN FIX THE PAIN IS THE ONE WHO CAUSED IT. JUST THINK ABOUT IT.

4] IT DOSENT MATTER WE TALK OR NOT THE OLACE I GIVE Y IN MY HEART WILL ALWAYS REMAIN SAME.

5] ONCE THE HEART GETS TOO HEAVY WITH PAIN, PEOPLE DONT CRY. THEY JUST TURN SILENT, COMPLETELY SILENT.

6] WHEN WE FIRST MET I HONESTLY HAD NO IDEA YOU WOULD BE SO IMPORTANT TO ME.

7] I AM A PERSON WITH NO PAITENCE. BUT IF I AM WAITING FOR YOUR REPLIES THEN BELIEVE ME YOU ARE REALLY SPECIAL FOR ME.

8] I SWEAR IT HURTS WHEN MESSAGES ARE SEEN BUT NO REPLY AND UNSEEN MESSAGES BUT ONLINE.

9] LOVING SOMEONE WHO DOESNT LOVE YOU IS LIKE WAITING FOR A SHIP AT AN AIRPORT. 10] YOU CAN REPLY ME AN HOUR, A DAY, A MONTH OR AN YEAR BUT I WILL REPLY YOU AS SOON AS I SEE YOUR TEXT.

The new generation that is the upcoming generation will be not knowing the feelings. When we talk about the word feeling the first thing which strikes our mind is the word LOVE. Great, actually this word has a more weightage, its beyond our imagination, it's the purest form of feeling etc.

now a days it has no value everyone will scare when they listen the word LOVE, especially parents will scare to the peak when they come to know that their kids are in love. Why, why this happened? It's all because of our generation.

Now a day's love is all about lust. They don't know the difference between LOVE & LUST.

In future generation it will be ruined more and more. Now I am going to tell a story which is narrated to a 23 years old boy by his father. Lets get into the story.

This is the story from year 2040.

There is boy named AKARSH. His age is 23. Studying engineering, who is crazy about girls, who is expert in flirting. He doesn't know the emotions, feelings. In one word he is a playboy. His father named VEDANT who is one amongst top 10 richest person in state, married to DIYA. She is a typical Indian woman and a homemaker. Akarsh is the boy who dated many girls and he neither girls were never serious about any relationship so far. Once he met a girl named Aarohi she is very pretty and she is so friendly with everyone. Aarohi is a junior to

Akarsh. And she didn't know the past life of Akarsh. During a college fest Akarsh saw Aarohi performing for a dance. He took a chance and made an appreciation for her performance. Akarsh got a chance to make friendship with her. As day passes, they exchanged numbers and started daily conversation. Text turned into calls and calls turned into video calls and as day passes meetings and outings has started. And slowly friendship converted into love. One fine day he made confession about his feelings and she took a time and accepted it as she didn't know about his past because he never shared with her. Everything was going fine and Akarsh completed his graduation he was not serious about his carrier because his father has much money. After his graduation he started to avoid Aarohi. She got confused about his behavior and finally without no reason he said a breakup for Aarohi.

It broke her heart and she went to depression and as a result she got failed in subjects. She couldn't able to digest her depression and failure and decided to end her life by committing suicide. She made an attempt to hang herself.

But is she lucky enough that her mother saw her hanging to fan and rescued her but it was bit late. She admitted to hospital, she was heavily injured around her neck and she had a laryngeal fracture, spine fracture, doctors informed that chances of being alive is less than 50%. She was kept in a ventilator and she is was in a death bed. Her father started to enquiry her friends to know the reason behind her suicide attempt. There he got to know about the breakup with Akarsh. He lodged an official complaint against Akarsh. Police began their enquiry and in no time, they arrested Akarsh. Vedant and diya had no idea about Akarsh arrest. Vedant used all his influence and got a bail for Akarsh.

After this Akarsh didn't understood one thing that how a girl can end her life for silly reason. Vedant came to know the stupid thing what Akarsh was doing till that day and he trashed him. He went to hospital to look the condition of Aarohi, it was very bad and he apologize to her parents. He convinced them and he shifted Aarohi to abroad for treatment, he took all the medical expenses and paid for it. Akarsh had one question left in his mind. And decided to ask her mother.

Akarsh:	mom, I need to ask you one question which is bothering me after this incident.
Diya:	ok ask me, I will answer.
Akarsh:	mom, what is love? Is that so serious?
Diya:	what you have done till today, that is not a love its only lust. You want to know the meaning of love? You want to know the depth of love? You want to know the purity of love? Go, ask your dad. You know one thing he is a not only a richest person but also, he is a greatest lover as I saw. Ask him

he will explain you. He is so ashamed of you today. Being his son, you did like this.

Akarsh: sorry mom.

Akarsh: waits for his father to return to home. He arrives, as soon as he arrived, he questioned his father.

Akarsh: Hai dad, I know you are ashamed of me, I am so sorry for what I did, I was not knowing that just breakup will be so serious.

Vedant :   oh "just a breakup". You fool its not just. You don't know the meaning of love so it is "just" for you. No, my son it's not as easy as you think. Till today you didn't experience the true love so you don't know the effect of it. Don't repeat it in future.

Akarsh :   no dad, I wont do it. But I wanted to know the real meaning of love, mom said to ask you. Can you please share that with me?

Vedant :   Ok come here take a seat. Diya you too take your seat. Akarsh you wanted to know the real meaning of love right ok let me tell you. Did you ever tried to think why I am so rich? No of course you didn't I know. Its because of love. Yes, you heard right. Love is not just meeting a girl, hanging out, chatting etc etc... love is an inspiration, motivation, understanding, sacrificing, pain, happiness etc etc etc. Ok let me tell you a story.

Akarsh :   a story, wow cool I am ready and excited to listen the story.

Vedant :   no, not just a story. It's the secret of my life which I never wanted to share with anybody. Very few know my story and in that few it includes your mom. Today I share this with you. But you should not just listen, you have to imagine and feel the characters then only it is possible to understand the beautiful concept love.

Akarsh :   Ok dad, I am ready.

(30 years ago-2010)

When I was at your age, studying engineering I was so joy full person I had no reason to get sad. I was enjoying my life to fullest I had no tension and I am not a brilliant student just an average student who is managing to pass all the subjects. Life was going easy somehow, I completed my 1st year of engineering. As we enter the second year, we became a senior so we were going for 1st year block and making fun of students and ragging them in fun manner. There I got a twist in my life. I saw a girl standing in a corner with innocent face, and very scared of seniors. As soon as I saw I was unable to take my eyes from her.

some kind of feeling started which I never experienced before. It called love at first sight.

Till I saw her I never believed the concept love at first sight. I was waiting to see her every day, I was waiting for my chance to talk with her. After a lot of research and struggle I got to know the name and branch. Her name was SARAH which means queen. Yes, she was like a queen.

Finally, I got a chance to talk with her after 4 months. I got a suggestion on facebook and I sent a friend request and she accepted. I wanted to text but my hands were freezing, I was unable to type but some how with all guts I texted her and got a reply. I was in cloud 9, I was so happy, no words are sufficient to describe my happiness on that time. I never wanted to stop conversation with her so I was texting her continuously and happy thing was I use to get a reply for my text.

This continued for about another 4 to 5 months. And decided to meet in college. Oh my god it was one of the best moments in my life. That night I didn't slept, I was waiting and waiting and waiting for sun watching clock continuously I was so excited. Finally, clock strikes 6 in the morning and sun was raising. I woke and started preparation to meet my queen sarah. Went to the college waiting for her near the cafeteria. I was there 1 hour before the decided time. I was well prepared to talk with her and had a fear that how to face her. I saw her arriving to cafeteria and in fear I hid behind the wall. She waited for 10 min and texted.

Sarha: hy Vedant where are you? I am waiting near cafeteria? are you busy right now?

Vedant: hello, I came to cafeteria 1 hour before but I scared to meet you and talk with.

Sarha: why are you so scared? Please don't make me embarrassed, come and take your seat.

With full of fear I went to her and took a seat. I greeted her with smile.

Sarha: are you okay now? Why are so scared, am I so ugly?

Vedant: hy no no no, you are gorgeous. The reason I am scared is I never talked with the girl before so.

Sarha: ohh ok its fine. I too never talked with the random guy this my first meet with a guy apart from class.

Vedant: so how the college life going on?

Sarha: yeah, it's good, how about you?

Vedant: yeah, its fine. How were your internals?

Sarha: can we please talk something out of academics?

Vedant: yeah sure, sure. I am sorry. I am tensed I don't know what to talk.

Somehow, I managed to talk with her we exchanged our thoughts and lifestyles and we exchanged a numbers. But never called her because I was a shy person. But I wanted share my feelings on her. I was waiting for a right time and texting continued for 2 years, even after 2 years I didn't get enough guts to say my feelings. I was scared of loosing her friendship too. I got my graduation completed.

I was knowing that if I leave college, I don't get a chance to see her in future and before leaving I wanted to see her one last time. I could have called her and ask to meet but I didn't because I was sure that I ending up in tears after saying an official goodbye to her. So, waited in the campus to see her after a long 1 hour waiting, she finally came to canteen, I was standing in one corner and watching her smile for one last time.

And as I said I ended up in tears and left her a message that I am busy so I couldn't meet her before going and said goodbye in text. Even after 3 years' time I couldn't express my feelings. I joined for higher studies but texting to her didn't stopped. After a year she completed her graduation too and got a job. Everything was going well and I left with one more year to complete my studies. Suddenly one morning I received a text.

Sarha: hai, I got engaged. Sorry I didn't invited you for an engagement because the exams are going on for you.

Vedant: hahaha…. stop kidding I know you are joking; you can't fool me.

Sarha: hy no, I am not kidding, I am serious.

Vedant: oh really, ok send me pics so that I can believe you.

Sarha: ok wait, see this is my fiancé.

[I received a bunch of pics] [I couldn't control my tears, I remained silent and staring her pics, cursing god]

Sarha: hy vedant you there?

[I dint replied her text because I was in shock and fear of losing her forever] After a lot of thinking finally decided to express my feelings to her I know it was already late but if I didn't try now, I know I will loose her forever. So, in the I called her.

Vedant: sarha, are you free now? I need to talk one important thing I need your time.

Sarha: yeah, I am free but is everything ok with you? Are you fine?

Vedant: yeah yeah, I am totally fine. I just wanted to say you the truth. Please meet me at river bed near our college, I am coming in 10 min its so urgent.

Sarha: yeah sure I will be there in 10 min. [I was waiting for her near river bed, she came and asked what happened] Vedant: Till today I just acted to be friend with you. I was never ready to be only friend with you. I can't loose you. I am nothing without you. [I went on my knees and confessed my love] look I waited for so many years for this right time. I don't know whether you will accept my love or not but I couldn't stop loving you. The first day when I saw you, right there I decided that you are my lifeline but I dint get a enough dare to confess, and if didn't tell you now I would end up by not expressing my feelings so I am confessing now please, will you accept my proposal?

Sarha: Vedant Look you are a very good friend of mine and you are an amazing person but you already know I got engaged. You have a bright future don't waste it. concentrate on your carrier. I wish to see you in very good position. Fullfill my wish please.

Vedant: what if I proposed before you getting engaged?

She left place by not answering my question. I cried and cried and cried on that day and I stopped texting her. It was very tough to avoid her but I have to do it. As she said I concentrated on my carrier to fullfull her wish and as a result I got placed in one of the top company with impressive salary package. I called to my parents and said about my placement they were so happy for me. After a long gap on that day I couldn't control so I texted.

Vedant: hai sarha, how are you?

Sarha: OMG, Vedant its been so long, I am good. How about you?

Vedant: yeah, I am good too. By the way I wanted to tell you that your wish is completed.

Sarha: My wish? What was that?

Vedant: your wish that you wanted to see me in good position, its fulfilled today. Thank you sarha for inspiring me. I am in this position because of my parents and you, thank you

Sarha: wow it's a great news we need to celebrate it and please stop being so dramatic ah. Saying thank you and all its more dramatic. I am so happy for you. I am bit busy I will call you tomorrow. Bye Like this again I started a conversation again and whenever I text her, I couldn't control my tears. Again, our daily conversation has started and again I was waiting for her call but I didn't receive any calls as usual she got busy with her work. But she was replying my text whenever she gets free time.

Finally, one day I got a call I was so happy and took a call. She said that she wants to meet so I dressed up and went to location where she already waiting for me.

Sarha: hai, was you busy, sorry I forgot to ask this before.

Vedant: no, I am never busy for my queen. Tell me what's the matter?

Sarha: vedant, you still waiting for me? Still loving me?

Vedant: [with vibrating voice] what type of question is this my queen? If you are in my mind I would have forgotten you by this time, but you are in my heart how can I forget my love towards you and fact is its increasing day by day and I will wait for you till my last breath, I know you don't have a feeling on me and I know I cant marry you but also I will wait for you.

Sarha: can you make one promise for me? Its last please

Vedant: anything for you my queen. If you will be happy from that promise then I wont event think twice to make a promise.

Sarha: few days ago, I met your mom and she explained about your decision and about your condition. You made a decision that you won't get marry? Please take back that decision and you have to get marry you made a promise and you can't break it.

Vedant: ok done I said anything for you, and I am ready to get marry. Its very difficult for me but all will be happy right if I changed my decision. Ok fine I am ready.

Sarha: thank you so much your mom already searched a girl for you and I already talked with her. We all liked her so tomorrow you are going to meet her.

Vedant: cool, ok fine.

Sarha: and one more thing very important after meeting her just meet me you have a surprise.

Vedant: ok fine done……

The next morning I went to meet a girl and I received a text from Sarha saying all the best..

Vedant: hai, I am Vedant how are you?

Diya: hai, I am Diya I am fine and nice to meet you…

Vedant: mom said that you liked me so straightly I will come to the point. I was loving one girl of course I am loving her now and I will do it in future you should not put any restriction.

Diya: she is Sarha right. Yeah she said everything about you and your feelings towards her and infact I liked you for that reason. You loved her beyond your ego, self respect, now a days this kind of love is quite rare and I am happy that I met that kind of person. I respect your feelings and I wont disturb them even in future. And about me I had no bad past nothing just simple living girl.

Vedant: are you sure? If yes then its good. Our parents will talk the further things. I take a leave now bye..

Diya: yeah I am sure. And I will be waiting to see us on our wedding album. Bye take care

After that all I was waiting for my surprise and Sarha came but she looked quite disturb.

Vedant: hai sarha,

Sarha: hai Vedant.

Vedant: why so late?

Sarha: sorry I was stuck in traffic, by the way how was the meeting?

Vedant: yeah it went good and I am doing this all only for you.

Sarha: thank you…. i am sure you will be happy in future.

Vedant: today you are looking so disturbed. What happened? Is everything fine?

Sarha: yeah yeah everything fine…

Vedant: so what's the surprise? I am waiting..

Sarha: [she handed over her wedding card to me] this is the surprise my wedding on coming month…..

Vedant: [tears started to roll down, I hid my tears controlled very hard] ohh wow cool it's a good news…I am happy for you….i am so excited…

Sarha: Vedant please stop acting I know you are not happy I can see your tears in your eyes so please control yourself. I am sorry vedant please don't spoil your life by remembering me. You have a beautiful life enjoy it. I don't want to see your life getting spoiled. Forget everything and move on.

Vedant: move on? Its so easy to say this word Sarha but its not gonna happen because I loved you with my whole heartedly and I am so serious about you. And you tell me to forget everything…. how? I don't understand how can I unfeel love once I have felt it? How can I forget that which gave me so much to remember? There is quote that "one bad chapter doesn't mean that the story is over" they say but why cant they understand that its difficult to turn the page when you know that someone wont be in the next chapter?

Sarha: but what about your future, what about you? I am scared about your future.

Vedant: why you are so scared? If you are happy then I will be happy. You smile when you are happy and I smile when I see you happy.

Sarha: I am scared because I LOVED YOU TOO

Vedant: what, what did you just say?

Sarha: yes you heard me right. I fell in love with you. How I can not love you when you are showing me so much love care respect. But I can't have you in my life. My mom wanted me to get marry with this boy and I don't like him, they didn't even asked me before engagement, didn't asked me before printing the wedding cards, and I am sure they wont ask me even now. Nobody wants my opinion. And I wont make my parents feel sad by stopping this marriage because they are everything for me. Till today they have done and sacrificed much for me and I owe them so I decided to get marry. But believe me I loved you the way you loved me.

Vedant: shall talk with them. Come lets go. I will explain them everything.

Sarha: no, its already too late and I don't want to hurt them now. Please can you sacrifice your love for sake of my parents.

Vedant: do you know how much I loved you? I can do anything for you and I can sacrifice my love for you. I want only one thing from you. Your happiness that's enough. I will do anything for your happiness you know that.

Sarha: I am sorry Vedant. Please take care.bye

And after this there was no conversation between us for month and one she texted me to come to marriage a week before. As she said I went a week before and she was happy.

[The night before marriage day we were talking in wedding hall]

Vedant: how's the preparation going on? Your parents will be very happy today.

Sarha: yes, they are happy.

Vedant: this is place where I wanted to sit and tie a knot around your neck. But tomorrow someone will sit on that place. From tomorrow you are wife to him. And there will no good morning, good night messages, I can't talk to you, I cant hear your voice, I cant make you smile I am going to miss you, miss your smile, miss your voice.

Sarha: I miss you too.

The time has come and she came and sat with him. She was looking gorgeous and I was staring her I couldn't take my eyes out of her. And again I fell in love with her. Every single moment we spent, we discussed was striking my head and I can see the first day when I met her infront of eyes. Then I realized that day dreaming is true, I experienced that. I was looking at her and all of the sudden she collapsed and everyone gathered around her but she was unconscious. I was blank I don't know what was happening. Her father came to me and said to drive her to hospital and I took my car and she was lying unconscious in back seat I took her to hospital with her parents and took her to emergency ward after some time doctors came out and said SHE IS NO MORE. Doctor explained that She died because of heart attack. It happens when people get depressed and when they can't handle the pain the heart stops the working.

By hearing this news, I collapsed on ground. After cremation I went to their house collected all her memories and asked her parents.

Vendant: are you happy now? You killed your daughter. Do you know that? You are the murders. you killed my love my Sarha. Why didn't you asked her before fixing her marriage? If you did then she would be alive now. Can you bring her back?

I cried daily for her. My room was filled with her pics and memories and when heart get too heavy with pain people just turn silent, completely silent. And after this all I married to diya as it was wish of sarha and we are happy together now but even now I didn't stop loving her. (Present day-2040) I still have that car in my garage and i can still see her on back seat. So my son this was the story of my love life which I loved her to the death and I couldn't get her. So respect the love, breakup is not a small matter.

Akarsh: now I realized that the true meaning of love. Dad can I see Sarha pics?

Vedant: come with me. See this is the secret of mine where nobody is allowed here. Today I am showing you. Look at this I created all her memories here and when I ever get sad, I spend some time with her.

Akarsh: dad I want to meet Aarohi. I will go to hospital.

[In hospital]

Akarsh: sorry uncle I made a big mistake how is she now? Aarohi's dad: [slapped Akarsh] she is still alive. Now please go out from here

Akarsh: I deserve this uncle but believe me I understood my mistake and came here to confess my mistake. Please allow me

[Aarohi from inside says "dad allow him"]

Akarsh: I am sorry Aarohi this was all because of me I won't repeat it please give me another chance to correct my mistakes. She allowed him to correct his mistake and now there are happily married and they blessed with the baby girl and named her as SARHA.

So a true love story is based on compromise, trust, respect. The pure love is when your smile because of someone, its special feeling. But when you cry for someone it's a love. You are so lucky if u receive first and last message of the day from same person. Every smile never shows a love but every drop from your eyes shows a trusted love.

So the meaning of title "the unexpected guest" here there are 3 unexpected guest.

1) Aarohi suicide: Akarsh didn't expected it. 2) Sarha: sarha entering the life of vedant. 3) Sarha death

These are "unexpected guest" in this story. So find your love. I am sure it will be so beautiful and it makes your life beautiful. Many peoples says bad things about love they talk when they don't deserve that or when they don't know the value of that.

As i said love is the inspiration it happened in vedant life. She inspired him to get into good position and she is the reason he is living his life and when comes to the sacrifice they both sarha and vedant sacrificed their love for her parents sake. And when comes to understanding divya did it well. When she knows everything about their love life but also she understood him and believed him and got married to him..

So the only message i like to convey through this story is love with your whole heart. Not with your hole heart. And parents, ask your daughter or son before fixing the marriage because they have lead their rest of the life with the life partners. Thank you all…

www.ingramcontent.com/pod-product-compliance
Lightning Source LLC
LaVergne TN
LVHW050424160726
843469LV00041B/1219